I0777000

Tall Tales of Transformation

Tall Tales of Transformation

First Edition: July 2025
ISBN: 979-8-9916539-0-9
E-Book ISBN: 979-8-9916539-1-6

Library of Congress Control Number:
2025909149

Joshua Spencer Keen
www.aweavingwizard.com

Odette Font by Canada Type

Tall Tales of Transformation

By A Weaving Wizard

As Told by Joshua Spencer Keen

CONTENTS

Dedication

To all those who are no longer with us,
especially my grand and great-grandparents
who gave me this spark long ago,
this is for you.

- Joshua

1.

Hello my beautiful Humans,
my dear wandering Souls,
the Time has arrived,
these Stories must be Told.

So come Gather round
and prepare your Ears to Listen,
for when this Wise Wizard Weaves,
We shall bring an End to Division.

2.

There are Deceiving Weavers twisting
Lies before our very Eyes.
Tumultuously tumbling through
Tall Tales until
the Talented Tumbler tumbles no more.

A Fountain of Feeling springs forward,
Its water washing Wicked Wishes
away. Vile Villains
transformed by Valorous Virtue.

The Deceiving Weaver's time is through
the Wise Wizarding Weavers are here for You.

3.

Powerful Winds are blowing,
the Seas have begun to Rise,
the Roots of the Earth trembling,
Fire burning in the People's eyes.

For the Guardians of the Realm
have awoken, Poised to lead
the Way. Guiding the People
to safety & the dawning of
a new Day.

4.

A Wise Wizard strolls,
humbly humming his way
through the Woods, as a peculiar Perspective
approaches, an intriguing Display of Goods.

This visage, a Vision,
the Eternal Tying of Tales, for in
this Knot Knit of Knowledge lay
the Holiest of Grails.

Foundational teachings were gifted
in Silent Celestial Symbol,
Now our Wise Wizard's finger
lies Housed in Hallowed Thimble.

5.

A wizard weaves, amongst the
falling of the Leaves, communing
consulting Celestial Creation, silently
soaking in a Forgotten Nation.

A wizard weaves, the Lamp
lying Lit within, barefoot & beholding
Boundless Beauty, clothed in colorful
crimson cloth.

A wizard weaves, chanting
cosmic calls of Elation, catalyzing
alchemical transfiguration. Sitting,
soaking in Sacred Source, the
finest Fibers flowing forth.

A wizard weaves, sewing with
Sacred Sinew, spinning soulful
substance into Silky
Seams, looming Life into
Linens of Love.

A wizard weaves, bowing
branches and twining twigs, vining
Virtuous Vision into a Templed Tapestry.

A wizard weaves with willful
Wisdom & Wonder, a Braiding
of Beatitude, a Blessed Thunder!

A wizard weaves for All
of Creation, telling Tall
Tales of Truthful Transformation.

A wizard weaves & It is
Time that We listen, for
We all Play a Role
in Its Grand Vision.

A Wizard Weaves...

6.

A Shepherd sits silently in the
Shade of the Yew Tree.
The Witching Wolves creep
closer to his cradled Flock.

Coordinated, crawling, Tongues
salivating in Proximity,
surrounding their tasty treats,
as the Imminent Instant inches
In.

Suddenly, a swooping
Celestial Spirit, a Staff
hammers the Earth,
a Roar rips through You,
Feeling like Birth.

A Reckoning rolling through
Reality, you can Run, but
It won't ease the Totality.

A Wave crashes, a Fire
burns, Earth alive with The
Breath of Life.

As Whimpering Wolves, now
Docile Dogs turn to Tend
their newfound Friends.

7.

Humble Humans gathering, a Vision
envisioned, igniting Inspiration & Innovation.

Dreams driven into overdrive,
their power pouring into physical form,
Majestic Magical Manifestation,
Words written & spoken for All
of Creation.

Designed to bring together
our Nations, Bearing this Fruit for All
our Populations.

So that We may Eat
from the Tree of Love.

8.

Articulating Artists,
alluding to aesthetic altitude,
alleviate Arrogance absolutely.
Like Archers aiming, precisely
pinpointing prime positions to promote
Peace.

Promulgating positive Presence amongst
Aristocratic Authorities, pushing these
Powerful Players to Promote this
Profound Platitude.

That Love is the Answer.

9.

Friendship forged in the
Fires of Fate, weaving Wisdom in
the Wandering of Ways.

There is no escaping this
Tying of Tales,
the Tribes are gathering,
blowing Thunderous Gales.

Their Voices will be Heard
from every Corner of the Earth,
to bring Truth to Power &
usher in re-Birth.

The Hour draws Closer,
the Hammer strikes Hard,
the People stand at the
ready, the Door left ajar.

Prepare yourself for Battle,
Bare your Totems & Gifts, through
the Eye of a Needle, Retribution will Be
Swift.

And when the Dust settles
and the People hoot Loud,
a new Morning shall awaken,
Bright, Brilliant & Proud.

10.

A damp Darkness dripping
slime across jagged Cavern walls,
as the Hero's torch flickers shedding Light
down Haunted Halls.

He hears the Beast bellow
a fearsome Roar from within,
but our Hero pushes onward Knowing
a Battle's soon to Begin.

As he rounds the Last Corner,
he can feel his Foe's breath,
he steps up to the Chamber,
Heart thumping in his Chest.

He charges through the Door!
Fearless, towards his Destiny!
But as he looks upon the Monster,
It's his own Face that he sees.

A stunned Second of Shock,
a Tumultuous Tussle ensues,
when suddenly It appears
our Great Hero is about to Lose.

It is in this Fateful Moment
that the Luminous Hammer hits,
Striking Deep our Hero
as the Illusion slowly lifts.

Our Warrior takes a Deep Breath, finally
able to Breathe, & Shattered
around his Feet, a Mirror,
Shadow's Illusory.

A Sacred Stillness settles
as he stands Straight &
True, the Angels croon a Calling,
their Soulful Light shining through.

Now I know you may not Believe me
but I Hope you Trust me
when I say, It is All of Ours
in every single way.

11.

If you Wander enough &
explore new Places,
searching Nooks & Crannies
for the most Sacred of Spaces.

You may find yourself
Empty, Disappointed & Lost;
on a late Flower's bloom
in the first Winter's frost.

But in the Revolving of Rounds,
a Shuffling of Hands,
Cards might be dealt
by Divinity's plans.

A sudden appearance,
a Feeling is Felt,
the Warmth of the Sun
hastening Spring's melt.

It is Here
in these Accidents,
these Unintentional Results,
that Magic moves Mountains &
Creation consults.

So have Faith in your Seasons &
Trust in Yourself,
allow the Journey to Unfold
& bring you True Wealth.

12.

The Faceless Forms of Fear's
treacherous Trickery, evoking
evasion, inciting invasion.

But none of this will do,
as Fear creeps ever closer,
Coming for You.

The Trick to this Game lies
within Nature, hidden
in Fear's name, disguised
Nomenclature.

A Silent Secret Sits in
Surrender, like a Surrounding Serenity
from an Unknown Sender.

So take a Deep Breath &
Find your True Center,
All it takes is a little Faith
& a Sacred Space you shall Enter.

13.

Divining Dreamers,
grounded in growth & rooted
through Rough Seas,
Join in Jubilation!

Communicate in Compassion with
Hearts wide open,
Orchestrate Soulful Symphonies,
Compose Ceremonious Circles!

Tenacious Tribes of Truth,
will you now
surreptitiously Sow your Seeds of
Saintly Spirit!

Will you Carefully Cultivate
your Crop of Creation,
re-route our reality
& recover an Old Road.

14.

The Earth trembles,
the People scream in Fear,
the Air is thick and poisonous,
an End draws Near.

The Water is black &
viscous, the Flames rise higher
& Higher. When all of a Sudden,
a Song is Heard,
cutting through Treacherous Desire.

It stirs the Soul that was
Slumbering, sleeping way down
inside, It soothes the Child's crying,
the Voice they thought was a Lie.

As the Song's amplitude accelerates
& a Celestial Choir joins in,
an awakening activates amongst them,
a vibration rising within.

A shift in Perspective is palpable,
a Revolution is about to Begin,
the People begin to recognize The
Meaning of the Word,
Kin.

That we are not so very Different after all,
as some would have us Believe.
And in this recognition,
a Remembrance,
the Gift of Love
We are ready to Receive.

And in this Receiving,
a Giving, Spread across the Earth.
The Grace of a Grateful Living
& all of the Blessings
It brings to Birth.

The Work wasn't easy
& there were times
the Treaties were tested,

But in the end
the People were Victorious,
Heart & Soul had their
Enemies bested.

The Boy was Spooked,
Lost in his Mind,
a Dilation of Time.

Scrambling & fighting
to Find his Way out, In
a last gasp desperate he screams out
a Shout.

Help! He pleads from down
on his knees, when the Winds start to Blow
& the Trees begin to Howl
& as sure as the Storm, he Hears
The Gnarliest Growl.

A Beast is approaching,
Gnashing his Teeth,
lumbering over to his Fleshy Feast.

The Boy is in Shock,
as still as could be,
Fate's cruel hand come to Deliver
his Day of Destiny.

When suddenly he Feels a Hand
on his Chest, a Spirited Clown
in Magical Dress,

Waltzing over,
grabbing this Beast by the horns,
flicking it one hundred feet
backwards, like Plucking a Thorn.

In the Flash of an Eye,
the Boy arises, as if Drawn
by Strings, his own Self
he surprises.

He stares around the Forest in Awe,
a Ball of Tears, it was
a Wise Wizard's touch which allowed him
to let go of his Fears.

He turns to meet his Savior,
exploding with Thanks!
but Finds only himself
along the Creek's banks.

He bows his Head low,
from the Earth to the Sky,
for this everlasting Memory will be his
Wings to Fly.

16.

Listen closely, the Time
has come, to Band together,
a Tribe of One.

You can hear Her
Calling growing louder in your Ear,
don't try to Ignore It,
don't Give in to Fear.

Just give yourself over
& Place your Faith in Her hands, for this
Voice that I speak of, is The
Mother, our Land.

There may be a Battle but
It's not what you Think,
for instead of the Other,
your own Poison you must Drink.

To Sit with your Darkness &
Face your own Shadow, Transfiguration
transpires in Footsteps, now
Hallow.

17.

A Rationalizing Register
ranting & raving,
consulting & compiling to satisfy
its Craving.

For Rules & Laws,
This's & That's,
always with a Trick
Tucked under its Hat.

Hiding its Purpose,
Disguising its Deeds,
Deception between the Lines
that it Reads.

A devious destruction
designed to attack,
coming for the Soul's throat,
a Knife in the Back.

But in the shifty Swapping
of Sounds, a Power appears
most Profound.

Love takes Hold & Begins
to work Its magic,
reversing a Fate that was
oh so Tragic.

And in its Place comes a Depth
of Understanding, Heart wide Open,
no such thing as Demanding.

Rolling & undulating the Fabric
of Life, reversing the Pain
& Suffering of Strife.

Rectifying Polarity,
Divining Division,
All things become One
in a Wise Wizard's vision.

18.

The Troll of Control,
The Troll of Control,
always exacting its Toll.

The Troll of Control,
The Troll of Control,
stumbling & fumbling,
crawling out of its Hole.

From under the Bridge he bumbles &
blunders, Yelling of Needs,
a Bellowing Thunder!

Hassling the Traveler,
Disturbing the Pilgrim,
belligerently berating all who come near
him.

Dictating Terms,
words written,
now Worms, decomposing &
rotting decisions, now Germs.

The Troll of Control,
The Troll of Control,
always exacting its Beastly Toll.

Until we See how
Foolish this be, for ever Believing
in this Conceptuality.

The Bridge doesn't exist
& neither does the Hole, in fact,
neither does the Troll
or the Traveler,
or the Pilgrim.

It's all just a Story,
like an ol' Mythic Rhyme,
Homer's words from an Ancient
Time telling Tall Tales of both
the Light & the Grime.

As the Vision vanishes,
a New Story begins,
One with the Source in Infinite
Origin.

So Open yourself up,
Hold up your Cup,
Allow that Love to come Roaring
Pouring Up.

Overflowing the sides &
rolling down your chin,
Give yourself the Gift of The
Graceful Grand Grin.

19.

Majestic movements of a
Magical Staff, waving & shaking,
trembling Its aft.

Fluttering through the Air,
Rippling the Reticulations,
rolling Its Love across the Nations.

The Prayers are said
in Orchestral Tone, the Tribe
drums a Beat, Harmonical Phone.

Calling the People,
Calling the Earth
to Rise Together,
to Bring about re-Birth.

The rebirth of the Land,
rebirth of Humanity,
because somewhere along the Way
We lost all our Sanity.

We pushed away Love,
We pushed away Soul.

Tell me,
Who sold you these Lumps of Coal?
Who Sold you this Smog,
these barren parking lots?
& What did you Give in Return?

Can't you Feel this Knot?
Deep in your Chest?
In the Pit of your Stomach?

The Earth burns
& We don't even Bat an Eye,
just roll on through
waving Goodbye.

But I am Here
to Tell you this is the End of this Lie.
This isn't a Game,
there won't be a Tie.

The People have come for the
Land that was Stolen & Return
to a Life that was Gifted, Beholden.

By the Heaven's & Star's,
we need not look very far
to See the Truth of these Poisonous Roots
that must be Ripped from the Ground.

A Sacred Purifying Bolt of Thunderous
Sound.

As the People chant loud,
standing tall & proud,
in what they have Become,
a New Day has Begun.

20.

I was the Beetle &
the Bard, the Chanting
Children from Afar.

I was the Land
the Buffalo roamed & the
fired Hearth in every Home.

I was the singing
Jesters of Old from whose
Lips all Stories were Told.

I was the Eagle spreading
wide & the Oak's limbs in
which Cardinals hide.

You See I Was
& Always Will Be, Now
Look Inside & Come
Join Me.

21.

The many Faceless Forms of Fear presents
A Formidable Foe.

Fortunately, this Visage is merely
a Vicious Illusion, Vanished
voluntarily by forging a foundation In
Faith.

The Torment of Tortuous Thoughts flounder
in the Fires of Illumination.

Alchemical transfiguration transpires
in Transparency & as sure as the Sun
Sets, Fear falls Back
into Balance.

22.

Paralysis, a Poisonous Vexation
of Spirit, the Soul's
death scream but you can
barely hear It.

Don't Fear It.
Breathe in & out,
Release your Doubt,
allow Presence to come about.

A Fount of Feeling,
the Ego reeling
as it Loses its Clout.

Without & Within,
let your New Day begin,
the Golden Chariot draws your
Graceful Grand Grin.

Tales as old as Time
told across the Lands,
Weaving together the People
found Hand in Hand.

A Plan emerges,
the Great River converges &
consolidates Its power.

The People must hold each Other
Close in these Final Hours.

As the Towers come crumbling
down, crashing & thrashing
Cinder to Ground.

The Spirits arise
from their Mythic Mound,
transforming a Landscape
with Teachings profound.

The Sound,
a Simplistic Tonality,
reshaping Reality,
the woven Cloth of Causality.

As Hidden in the Loom,
Mercury's shuttle Graces Humanity from
Doom.

Held by but a Thread from
the Land of the Dead,
the rebirth of the Living in the
Great Dreamer's Head.

23.

A Flick of the Pen,
a Twist of the Quill,
the Sultry Sounds speaking
of Will.

A yearning of Heart,
a pouring of Soul,
to Mend the Fabric,
Turn the Tapestry Whole.

The Tone of the Twill
& the Sinew's Sojourn,
Heart-filled substance spills
from the Urn.

A Holy Rite
of Ceremonial Healing
as the Deepening delves
to uncover True Feeling.

A reeling of Mind,
Lost in Time,
forgotten Its place in
Old Mythic Rhyme.

Seeing the Signs,
Heart & Soul climb, from their Roots
in the Ground to their Home
most Profound.

As the Sun & Moon meld
into One, the People
toil Together & a New
Tale is Spun.

24.

A Thought,
a Feeling,
a Word,
a Pen,

Thoughts so many, Transmogrify -
a Cooped up Hen,

But then,
in the midst of this Struggle,
the Hustle & Bustle abruptly...
comes to an End.

And as We turn
to Find that Silver Line of
the Middle Mind,
the Thumping Conductor
of a Plan Divine, Thoughtless
Mastermind bleeding red hot Love
throughout All of Time.

So give yourself this
Blessing, a Lesson in
Radical Self Love,
Acceptance.

The Time has come,
our Truth will set us Free,
a Leap of Faith in Mind,
Illusory.

And as we Be, the Universe
was always inside
you & me, Giving the
Land of Milk & Honey.

25.

Bejeweled waters whispering
Below, all the Secrets
seemed to Know.

Above on high
the Eagles fly, Perspective's
sight of the People's cry.

They die & suffer, anguish,
trampled, torn asunder.

The Blunder of the West's
ways, Ego's proclamation of
a better day. But for whom &
for what?

Short-sighted Men
with Heads in their Butts.

For who is to say
it's better this way,
when the Earth was a Gift
& the People played.

They Danced & they Sang &
they Wrang from Life
every Drop of Joy.

Come now Brother,
there's no need to be Coy,
We see your Ploy.

Your Vile Visions,
your Plans of Division,
the Words of Derision's
Venomous Mission.

Conditioned,
Divide & Conquer,
but no longer,
We start to Strut & Saunter.

Voices found amidst
the Circular Round, the Time
has come for the People's Crown,

To be laid on the Head,
as the Tribes break Bread,
Destiny re-written,
Healing the Dead.

26.

The Glowing Fire of the Ancestral Mind gifts
all Blessings in due Time.

Rhymes in lines Past,
Present & Future,
the scriptured word or
the shaman's suture.

Mending the Bonds that were
Torn & Frayed,
Journeying in,
Fate they Prayed.

For safe Passage & Return
of the Soul, the Power
to Turn the Tapestry
Whole.

27.

Polarity pervades
this Prismed Perspective, as the
World sways, ebbs & flows.

From here to there,
Out to In,
osmotic diffusion,
Yang & Yin.

Highs to Lows,
convective cycles,
re-birth, Water's cascade
cleansing the Earth.

The People dance in Solar Array,
an old Game with many Names,
Symbols we Play.

Mirrored ways of Magic &
Might, forging Foundations,
Shadows to Light.

A glimpse of a Whisper beckons you
Home, Soul's Song sung in stars
astral dome.

28.

Settle down,
Find your Breath,
Reach out for the final Step.

Go around the Circle
& then a Left.

For there comes
a Time when All
your best, floats around & flies on
through, leaving you Stumbling, questioning
Who?

A You of which All comes
to Bloom, Unfolding within the
Mother's Womb.

The Cosmic Father calls his
Grace, Awakening your True Face.

The Boundless Space deep
within Draws up the
Grateful Grin.

An inspirational Whim of Form
& Shape. A logically clever little
Great Ape.

A Drape of Symbols in
the Performer's nimble Hands,
the People's incantation giving
Praise to the Land.

To Journey back Home,
there's no need for a Plan,
just Remember the Truth of Being,
I am.

29.

You must Die &
Bare one thousand Deaths
as Grace falls,
your final Step.

Passing the Threshold
to the Other side,
the Eternal Fire's
Celestial Ride.

A Guide through the
Land of the Night,
leading the Soul through
the Most Fearsome of Fights.

A Gift of the God's will come
to be Found, in Rhythmic
Fashion, circling round.

Profound & Absurd,
a Call will be Heard
by listening closely
to the Whispered Word.

For as sure as the Song
of the Siren's at Sea,
this Journey will bring you
down on your Knees.

As you Plead to Be
Shown the Way,
out of the Darkness &
into the Day.

Praying for Blessings &
Fears allaying,
God arises, shifting
in Steady Formless Staying.

Lighting the Lantern
cradled Within,
the Journey Home is
Set to Begin.

Hand & Hand
with the Loving Land,
back at the Doorway,
I take one final Stand.

To look around,
Drink as much as I can,
to Remember the Truth
of this Being, I Am.

And in a Step,
the Forest appears,
after One Thousand Journey's
I am finally Here.

A Weaving Wizard,
with my staff & my hat,
transformation transpires
Just like That.

30.

I want to Sit &
Listen to the Trees,
& all the things
they have to Tell.

I want to Sit &
Listen to the Breeze
with all the whispers
that lift our wings.

I want to Sit
& Listen to the Water conduct
teachings of flow,
emerging from veiled depths.

I want to Sit
& Listen to the Dancing
Warmth as the People gather
round.

I want to Sit
& Listen to the People,
their pain, their suffering,
heavy hearts & twisted minds.

To know what is
so that We may
See, inside & around
this Branching Tree.

31.

To & fro,
come & go,
beautiful Poetry for those who
Know.

The Sound of Grasses greening,
the Song & Shimmer
of Starlight's meaning.

A Feeling,
Ignored by most, yet
inhabiting all
like some Holy Ghost.

From coast to coast,
sea to sea,
Everything is Found
Inside a We.

Multitudinous masses,
cantankerous clashes,
absolving ashes,
Timelessness passes.

Into an Age of Fire &
Rage, Fear finally let out
of Its cage.

Destined to destroy,
a scared Little Boy,
mischievous malevolence
of a malicious ploy.

But All is the Same
in this Particular Game.
Fortune, Fame,
Blame or Shame.

For whatever it is
will be Laid to Rest,
to let one's self go
is to Pass the Test.

To rise again,
Earth Water & Fire, is to know
the Truth, Heart's greatest Desire.

So come on in
& Settle down, it's Time
We start another Round.

It's okay to Play & have Fun
in the Game, Destiny is
Written by Many Names.

32.

A Blizzard,
a flurry of fortuitous woes,
the Heat Engine's pumping,
the Body that Grows.

It knows
the final destination, but
must still make a Stop at
every Station.

Elation's Oration,
Pronunciatory Power!
The Emphasis,
Elective's drawing Hour.

Purpose & pride with
no Where to Hide,
Surrendering in,
a humbling Guide.

A Forgiving of Fate
served on a Plate,
taking ourselves on
Destiny's Date.

33.

There once was a little boy,
an intense, fiery, passionate
Little Boy.

Now this little boy was often
misunderstood, the World tried to
tell this little boy who he was,
& what he was,
was wrong, all Wrong.

And for a Time, a Long Time
in fact, this little boy believed
these Lies, he believed all the ways
his little boyish self needed Fixing.

But the Truth is,
we've all been misled.
No little boy or girl is ever born Broken
or Imperfect
or Born any other way
than the way they Are.

And it was on this Journey,
this path called Life, with all its Pain,
and all its Suffering,
& its Joys,
& its Happiness,

that this Little Boy was finally able
to See all of the Magic
that he was a part of.

Woven into every Thread &
Cell & Fiber of his Being.

And little by little,
this Little Boy was able to break
every chain he thought the world had
laid upon him.

Until one day,
he was finally Free,
now destined to become
the man he was
Born to Be.

Wings spread wide amid the Smiling
Sky, the World used
Its Trick to Teach this Little Boy
How to Fly.

34.

How do you Speak
to a Heart, when Words & Thoughts fall
Short?

And not by a little, but by a Mile,
a Stretching Chasm,
an Abyssal Depth reaching
as far as the Eye can See.

Perhaps It starts by humming
a Humble Tune, like One would
on a Sunny Day while Waiting
for an Old Friend to Arrive.

Or perhaps, It comes like the Birds
at First Light of Day. Naturally,
as if It were always Present,
as if some Song had Sprung into Being
with the very Creation of the Universe Itself.

And Its Melody slowly wafting,
washing Its way across

some Immeasurable Shore, to Find
a Heart that had once Forgotten,
the very Song Its own Self
did Make.

And as the First Chords
Strike upon its Breaches, a trembling
Resonance awakens. A Thumping
Rhythm, that sounds & resounds in the
very Chapels of its Solitude.

Its once Cold Keep,
now again an Amphitheatre
for the Chorus of the Universe,
and the whole World,
a Stage.

For how do you Reach a Heart?
I'm not quite sure, but
a Song may be a Good Place
to Start.

<u>Acknowledgements</u>

To all those who helped me along the way,
Thank you <3

To my family and friends,
your support through this process means
more than you will ever know.

To everyone,
this thing was never mine,
for the keeping belonged to the
Great Dreamer's sleeping.

Written as much for me as by me.
Thanks for reading!

- Joshua Spencer Keen

<u>Epilogue</u>

A Blind Man serves,
a Blind Man leads,
a ragged Band across
The Mystery Sea.

Waves tossing,
to & fro,
slowly making,
a Way unknown.

To many & most,
but not All,
The Wind whispers
a Silent Call.

Filling the Sails,
drawing Them on,
the Ship rolls
from Dusk to Dawn.

Treacherous torrent,
pitched, a lean,
held for dear Life,
Love unseen.

Till at last,
the Eye is met,
burning away
Illusion's net.

Calmer currents
come, prevail!
Drifting Home by Heart
or Tale.

Footsteps meet
the old Seashore,
Love returned at last,
Once more.

- A Weaving Wizard

Some space for your thoughts...

I loves ya :)